To Save a Soul

ANGELIA DESANZO

Copyright © 2017 Angelia DeSanzo
All rights reserved
First Edition

PAGE PUBLISHING, INC.
New York, NY

First originally published by Page Publishing, Inc. 2017

ISBN 978-1-64027-318-4 (Paperback)
ISBN 978-1-64027-319-1 (Digital)

Cover by Aaron Jones

Printed in the United States of America

Chapter 1

The sun was setting on a hot August Arizona night. I climbed to the top of Camelback Mountain to view the magnificent burst of colors that sprayed across the horizon. I had always loved the sunsets in the west, the way the world looked so innocent right before dark. I had grown fond of the sunsets here in Phoenix, and I was convinced that this was one of the prettiest places on earth.

I appreciated the beautiful scenery because I was not a native. I grew up in a small town in western Pennsylvania, where it was cold and dreary for about eight months out of the year. And even though I missed the snow around Christmastime, the sunsets every night made up for the winter wonderland. I was only nineteen when I uprooted myself from a world that seemed so distant now.

I felt so trapped and inhibited my whole life. I knew I had more to offer the world, but sometimes I wished I wouldn't have listened to my wandering heart that yearned for the wild Wild West. I was a teenager, with my head in the clouds. I had no clue how lonely I would be once I picked up and left everything I ever knew. All I wanted seemed so simple. I wanted to see the sun shine every day, and I wanted a fresh start. However, it wasn't soon that I found no matter how far I ran, I couldn't run from myself!

As I reached the top of the mountain, I took a deep breath and let out a fierce scream. I was trying to let out the steam of another stressful and degrading day I knew as my life. I ran my golden-brown fingers through my bleach-blond hair and sat on the desert dirt beneath me. As I dangled my feet over the mountain, I gathered rocks in my hands and began dropping them as though I was dropping quarters into a slot machine. As I watched the rocks fall hundreds of feet, thoughts of terror filled my troubled head. My soul began to wrestle with my mind about the decisions I had made, and with my head in my hands, I broke into tears.

To everyone else I was a fiery, brave, beautiful young girl, but to myself I was a waste of beauty and talent. As my body trembled with self-hate, I screamed out to the rest of the world, "How the hell did I get here?" I sat almost motionless as I was waiting for an answer, but the only reply was from my own mind: "You did this." I played memories over and over in my head like records. It seemed I had given up everything that was ever important to me for a material object, the root of all evil, money! The one thing in my life I thought was harmless had destroyed my self-worth and created an overwhelming dependence, and now my pride was the only thing I wanted to walk away with. But at twenty-two years old, my life seemed easier to take than to change! With tears clouding my vision, I wiped the dust off my shorts and prayed that God would forgive me for all my sins, especially the one I was about to commit!

My mind then went to the heartbreaking call I had received earlier in the day! My dear sweet Sean, my friend who had been my rock, was dead at twenty-eight! Why God took angels on earth boggled my swizz cheese soul!

I was so sick of all the evil that plagued me, and even though all through Catholic school I was taught that if you committed suicide you would go to hell, I still felt it was the only way out. I figured, "What's the difference? I make deals with the devil here on earth every day, so why not spend eternity with him? Besides, where has God been for the last four years? Where was His guidance when I needed it the most?"

I closed my eyes and pictured my family's faces when they learned of my fate. I was the oldest of three, and I was definitely the rebel in the family. My parents were both retired marines with very conservative views. I, on the other hand, always appreciated the abnormalities in life. At the early age of three, I was fascinated with nudity and wondered why anyone had to wear clothes.

I knew my parents would be upset when they heard of my fate, but they were always too preoccupied with their new spouses and their new lives. My brothers and I just seemed to be a bad reminder to their pathetic marriage. Besides, they never really took the time to know me, or they would have realized the severe depression that I had been going through. The only person that I didn't want to hurt was my grandmother. I always felt she was the one person that truly loved me, and I would miss her the most.

My body shook with anxiety, and a voice in the back of my head said, "I am here, don't do it," but that was just my conscience; and in the last four years, I got pretty good at drowning that voice out. Besides, what was the point of listening to it now? I knew people think it is selfish to kill yourself, but I was the only person I was living for. I felt Earth was the cruelest place to live, for being an exotic dancer, I saw it all.

I never liked to refer to myself as a stripper because I was a topless entertainer, and I hated all the negative stereotypes that the word stripper immediately conspires in the minds of most. I felt the term exotic dancer painted a better picture of me, because in the beginning, I saw dancing as a form of eccentric art. I was blind to the filth that filled "strip" clubs. And no matter how nice the club looked on the outside, the core of all clubs was disgustingly dirty and basically the same. Smoke filled rooms slightly lit, full of people either spending money or earning money, fulfilling a desire or desiring to be more.

And when I say I saw it all, I meant it, for I lived in the coldest form of reality. I saw the dark and deceptive side of all men and women, you know, the side their mothers or wives never saw!

In my earlier days, I partied with the rock stars and athletes, snorted cocaine with the lawyers and doctors, and broke bread with the politicians and the cops. And while society frowned upon me for my job, they worshiped all these men who were the sole reasons these clubs existed.

And just the thought of men made my stomach turn. I actually used to feel bad for their wives, who were home tucking their kids into bed, while their deceitful spouses were tucking their paychecks into my garter. So after the initial glitter and glam wore off, I was left with the reality of people's true intentions when they enter into that elusive world. And the realization of what I was selling there was so sad I could only deal with it in three ways: shots, lines, or pills.

By the time I realized my job was the root of most of my problems, I was in way too deep! By my nineteenth birthday, my bills were more than four grand a month. I no longer wanted to do this job; I had to. I was way too proud to run back to Daddy, and I'd rather die than admit that the girl that once got into MIT was a failure. As my emotions turned from sorrow to rage, I made the only decision I was ever sure of. I no longer wanted to be looked at like a piece of meat. I no longer wanted to be judged from the outside in. Today would be my last day!

Chapter 2

I struggled to stand; my knees were knocking together so hard I almost fell over. But from deep inside, I gathered what I thought was courage, felt the earth beneath me for the last time, and with no regrets, soared into the sky!

My body plummeted toward the rocky ruble while my soul rose above. My 125-pound frame hit the ground at about thirty miles an hour. My once-healthy bones shattered inside my skin, while blood sprayed from my mouth like it was coming from a faucet. CeCe Marco was no longer human; I now only was a spirit that lingered in the sky, waiting for the consequences of my desperate actions. I couldn't believe I had just witnessed my own death. I was emotionless, like

I had just watched a scene from a cheesy horror movie. I was floating in the sky, and I wondered if I was visible to the human eye. I was suspended in midair, and the earth was a like a movie that I was watching. Everything happened so fast that I wasn't sure if I was dead or I was dreaming.

But in one split second, the movie theater grew darker and darker until all my surroundings became totally pitch black—a color black my human eyes had never experienced—and a voice echoed in the distance. I no longer felt the shame and sorrow of my life. How could I? I no longer had a human body, which meant I no longer had a body to sell for money.

Death, on the other hand, was nothing like I thought it would be. There was no shining white light that welcomed me to the Garden of Eden. I didn't feel angels around me either. All I could hear was a voice in the distance, and the voice was becoming louder. I couldn't make out the words or even if the language I was hearing was English, but I was sure the words were being directed to me. For the first time since my death, I grew scared. I closed my eyes, only to reopen them to what looked like an older black man with a white outline around him that made him look ghostly.

"Don't be frightened, my child, for fear you have not even experienced yet." He sounded as though he had a Southern accent.

"Who are you?" I called.

"Who do you think I am?" he answered.

Since I was filled with so much fear, or that's what I thought, I was certain I was speaking with Satan himself.

"That's funny," he replied. "You always thought the gifts I gave you came from some deep dark place. You never stopped to think your beauty or talents came from me."

I stood there speechless because he had just read my mind. After what seemed like an eternity, I found the nerve to speak.

"So you are God?" I questioned.

"Oh no, I am not your interpretation of God either."

I stood confused and frustrated. I mean, if I was dead and he wasn't God or Satan, who was the deity I spent my whole life worshiping and fearing?

He interrupted my thoughts. "Who I exactly am is not important right now, but for your sake, you can call me Othello. You will learn very soon why I was sent to you and why you are worthy of neither God nor Satan yet."

I still felt like I was floating, and I even tried to pinch myself to see if I was dreaming, but I had almost no feeling left in my arms.

"Your soul has been worn very thin. That's why you do not feel complete."

"How do you know how I feel?" I said in a snappy tone.

"My name might be Othello, and I appear to you as a man, but that does not mean I am one."

"I never said you were one," I replied hastily.

"No, but you are intimidated by me, and your tone shows it."

Me intimidated by a man? I thought. No. Men never intimidated me. In fact, it used to thrill me that tiny innocent me often intimidated them.

"Forgive me for my tone," I said. "I just thought death would bring me joy, and so far it has just brought me you!"

"Trust me, CeCe, death will soon bring you a lot more. Be happy it brought you me, for things could be much worse. Everything from now is all up to you."

"Well, if it's up to me," I said cheerfully, "I want to be with all the angels. I want to sit on fluffy white clouds, and I want to see my grandfather and uncle who have already passed."

"So is that why you killed yourself?"

"No, I did it because I hated the pain I felt every day, the feeling of regret that overwhelmed me."

A dead silence fell all around. Othello looked deep into my green eyes and stood quietly as if he was pondering ideas. I knew I had only just met him, but I trusted he would not do me harm.

"I have been given many powers, and one of those powers is to help repair souls. Souls that are worth repairing, that is. I want to give you back your life when your soul was intact, but I need you to want this also," he responded.

"You can read my mind, so what do you think I want?"

Othello shot me a look of anger and disgust, and with no warning, I felt tiny creatures crawling all over me, and a strangling like a python was squeezing me. I tried to scream, but when I opened my mouth, the only thing that came out were spiders. Hundreds of them poured from my mouth like blood squirting from an open flesh wound.

"Are you ready to cooperate?" Othello yelled.

"Yes," I retorted, "just please remove these horrible creatures."

Snakes, spiders, and basically anything that crawled were my biggest fears when I was living, and apparently that hadn't changed.

"My dear," Othello said with sympathy, "if you do not want to cooperate, that is your destiny, for eternity!" "Remember, you do have choices here."

In a frightened tone, I asked, "Speaking of here, where exactly are we?"

"You are where you were on Earth, only a few miles above. Your body is still lying as you left it while your soul is hanging in the balance," he explained. "Many humans refer to this place as purgatory. However, it is not exactly that."

"Now," he murmured, "that we're clear on that, are you ready to start repairing your soul?"

"Yes, but what happens after that?" I asked.

"I forget how impatient you are." Othello chuckled. "That has not been decided for you yet. To repair your soul, I have to take you back to a time when you listened to your heart, but remember one thing. Just because you are going back, that doesn't mean everything will be the same, or that you are supposed to change everything either. Some choices you made on earth were simply written in your chart, so you had no power to ever change them! I simply just want you to listen to your heart! It will tell you when you are right or wrong."

"I don't really understand," I muttered.

From a distance, he blew me a kiss that surrounded me with warmth. He replied, "Don't worry, you soon will!"

Chapter 3

All of a sudden the utter blackness that I had become familiar with transformed into the room I had spent most of my teenage years in. Here I was, standing in my bedroom at my father's house. I ran over to my full-length mirror that hung on my closet door. I was mesmerized when I saw my reflection. I stood there for almost fifteen minutes, studying myself.

My hair was its natural dishwater blond. I knew I had to be no older than fifteen, because at sixteen, I lightened my hair to the color of Marilyn Monroe's. My locks were shorter and curlier than I ever remembered it being, but it was cute. It's funny that I now thought it was cute when I had spent my teenage years hating my appearance. Here I was, starring face-to-face with the kid I spent years trying to forget.

My walls were full of the normal teenage girl posters. I forgot how much I loved Dennis Rodman until I was reunited with the wall-size poster I had of him. I looked all around my room with curiosity. I felt such a sense of contentment.

I walked over to my dresser to go through my drawers, when I felt a stab in my foot.

"Ouch!" I cried out. I looked down to realize a piece of glass was stuck in my big toe. Where did this come from? And like a crash of thunder, it hit me. This had happened before! I wished it were just a bad case of déjà vu, but I had to face reality; I was reliving one of the worst days in my life.

I sat on my bed and pulled the piece of glass out of my foot. It came from a picture I had thrown at the wall the night before. The picture was of Thad and me. Thad was my first love and my first everything!

I didn't have to look at the calendar because I already knew the date, but just to make sure, I glanced at the one on top of my stereo. February 10, 1996, it read, and I broke into tears.

A month earlier I learned I was pregnant, and this was the day I was to terminate the pregnancy. I was fifteen years old and having to make literally a life-and-death decision, one that for me would just contribute to the many that I would forever regret.

I had been dating Thad, who was almost five years older than me, for about a year now, and we had the perfect relationship. We were so in love, with so many plans for the future, but a baby right now wasn't possible. I always knew Thad was the person I one day wanted a family with, and I figured one day it would happen. It broke my heart that I had to give this baby up, but I wasn't even old enough to drive a car, let alone raise a child.

My pregnancy was a total secret. I lived with my father, and I was afraid he would kick me out if he knew. The only people that knew about the pregnancy besides Thad and me were my mother and his sister, Raquel.

The only reason I even told my mother was because in 1994 Pennsylvania indicted a state law that required parents' permission for an abortion in anyone less than seventeen years old. My mother, a religious Catholic, did not believe in abortions, but she believed in my future! She felt I would never go to college if I had the baby, and she desperately wanted to see me make something out of myself. As my mind wrestled with my heart, I was interrupted by a familiar sound.

Beep, beep. Thad's car horn blasted in the driveway, and it scared me half to death. I lifted my bedroom window and yelled out, "Be right there!" I was so excited to see him.

He looked just the way I remembered—short curly brown hair, chestnut-brown eyes, masculine steel arms, and the most beautiful full lips I would ever see. Thad was my perfect mate! He had a heart of gold and the reputation of a saint.

He grew up in the typical American family. His family consisted of a hardworking father, a loving stay-at-home mother, and a beautiful older sister. I, on the other hand, grew up in a more modern family. My parents divorced when I was nine, and I decided, along with my oldest brother, to live with my father. Every time my parents even tried to have a conversation, it would end in a world war two fight. But despite our very different upbringing, Thad and I felt we were one.

I threw on some baggy sweat pants, pulled my hair in a ponytail, and ran down to meet him. By the time I got outside, my mom was there chatting with Thad.

"Are you ready to go?" replied my mother quietly.

"Ready as I'll ever be," I replied, holding back tears.

My mother and I never really talked about the major decision I was making or how it was going to affect me.

The car ride was pretty quiet. Thad held my hand the whole way to Pittsburgh. We only lived about forty miles north of Pittsburgh, but the car ride felt like we were on a cross-country trip.

"CeCe, you know I love you. If you don't want to do this—" Thad started.

"No," I interrupted, "I am sure."

Inside though I was killing myself. Here I was. Othello was giving me a second chance. Wasn't I supposed to listen to my heart? And my heart wasn't being logical. It was saying, "Keep this baby because it is a love child." I always wished I could have this day back, and here it was, but it wasn't how I pictured it.

For years I regretted having the abortion because I believed it was the beginning of the end for Thad and me. I blamed him for my shame, and I slowly pulled away from him because I associated the abortion with him. It took me years to figure it out, but I always believed that if we'd had the baby, we would have shared a beautiful life together. But as we were driving to the clinic, I realized if Thad and I were meant to be, we would be. The abortion should make us stronger. I never expected to feel this way given a second chance, but then again, things are never the way you imagine them to be.

The wind was bitter, and light snowflakes danced on my hair as we walked from the parking garage to the clinic. As we rounded the block, I was astonished at what I saw. There had to be at least fifty picketers surrounding the entrance to the building. I took a deep breath and almost collapsed to the ground.

"Be strong, CeCe," Thad commented.

"Just ignore them, dear," sounded my mother.

Out of the blue, this woman in a yellow shirt approached me and grabbed me by the arm.

"Don't worry, I am here to protect you. I am a staff member from the clinic," muttered the woman. The fact that I needed protection began to spook me.

She accompanied us until we were safely inside the clinic. The number of protesters amazed me, and I was utterly appalled by the un-Christian things these holy people were shouting at me. One man even told me I deserved to die on the table. If I wasn't so sad about the whole situation, I probably would've hauled off and hit him.

The look in Thad's eyes was all I needed to keep me strong. I felt so secure with him, and as they called me back, I couldn't believe I was going to kill what we created. Our eyes never left each other as I was led into the death chamber. As the glass door closed between us, he blew me a kiss good-bye.

My body filled with anxiety, and I was scared. The physical pain was the greatest I ever experienced. My mother wouldn't let them knock me out for the procedure because she couldn't take me to my father's house drowsy when he thought we were just shopping!

Tears flooded my eyes because I was more confused this time than before.

"Are you all right, dear?" questioned the nurse who was leading me to the room where the surgery was scheduled to be performed.

"I am fine, thanks for asking," I retorted.

The room was the size of an office cubicle. Two doctors entered shortly and told me to get completely undressed. As they placed my legs into the stirrups, they began to explain the procedure.

"This surgery will only take four minutes after everything is properly inserted," said one doctor. The other doctor remained by my side and told me to squeeze her hand as hard as I needed.

Rods that ranged from one to five inches were then inserted in the walls of my vagina. To try and remove myself from the reality of my situation, I turned my attention from the doctors to the pale yellow wall to the right of me. Out of nowhere, the wall became a television, and Othello was the star starring back at me.

"Listen to your heart, my child," was all he said, and then he was gone again.

I gathered my thoughts, and as the doctor turned the vacuum-sounding, life-sucking machine on, my heart cried out.

"No, no, I can't do this. This isn't the decision that my heart wants," I said sternly.

And with just those words, the whole scenario changed. The doctors broke into tiny particles and vanished like dust in the wind right before my eyes.

Chapter 4

I lay in astonishment with nothing but my hospital gown between me and the cold wind that whipped over my body. Utter blackness once again filled the once-awfully light clinic room. Othello appeared before me at the end of my hospital bed.

"What happened to the doctors?" I questioned.

"They are where they're supposed to be—gone! Just like the past, my dear," he said grimily. He must have known the sheer pain I was in, having to relive the day I was a mother and in the same a murderer!

"See, you were just reliving a memory, not real life," Othello began to explain. "I was sent to you because you were once a true human, a woman who listened to her heart, her soul. Somewhere down your bumpy road, you stopped listening, and your soul slowly faded away. And only you can decide which road you will follow after all your pieces are put back. You made the right decision by refusing the abortion, not because of your prolife choice, but because you listened to your inner self."

His words were so sincere. I felt so at peace with myself whenever he spoke. I only wished his words of wisdom would have accompanied me when I was alive. I had so many bizarre and vivid dreams after the procedure, and I wondered why he just didn't come to see me in my sleep. Maybe if he did, I wouldn't have felt so hopeless.

"I know you are wondering why it took killing yourself to get spiritual help, but God has given all of us free will. He expects all of us to make choices out of love," Othello remarked. Here he was, once again reading my mind. "When a person commits suicide, they cut God's plan short, so even He is shocked," he expressed with much desperation in his eyes.

"I know on earth you heard stories like when it thunders, it's God bowling, and when it rains, it's God crying. Well, part of that is true. Rain is God's tears. Each raindrop stands for a person who's just chosen not to follow God's plan."

"So right now on Earth, it is raining?" I asked.

"Yes," Othello replied, "somewhere on Earth rain is drenching the treetops with God's sorrow for you!"

For the first time since my suicide, I felt totally selfish for killing myself. I never knew I was important, that God actually had a plan for me.

Othello must have felt my shame. He rested his gentle hands on mine and said, "I think it is time for you to start forgiving yourself."

Inside I really did want to heal my heart. I yearned for forgiveness for many years, but every time I would try to deal with my regret, I would only end up going through the pain all over again. Then one day I made a pact to never think of it again, but somewhere in the darkness of my dreams, I would hear a baby crying, and all the disgust would come back. Before I could even explain, Othello interrupted.

"You were going to miscarry that child. That life was never meant to be," he answered. "You will see that soul again one day if you do the work that is before you now!"

"What?" I sounded off in disbelief.

"It wasn't the right time for that soul to be born, but God was trying to teach you a lesson about life and love," Othello remarked.

"Why would God put me through all of that turmoil for nothing?" I said. A crippling sensation of the unknown seemed to rip right through me.

"You're missing the point. Everything has significance," he answered with unquestionable sincerity. "Humans don't understand the mystery of life, yet they try and control it. You prayed every night when you found out you were pregnant, and God was listening. You just didn't give Him a chance to work His magic. Instead, you took matters into your own hands, and for the rest of your life, you blamed yourself, Thad, and even your mother. That decision permanently damaged your soul, causing much of the self-hate and need for constant physical perfection."

It all made so much sense. I cried so violently that even Othello's usual nonchalant eyes filled with comfort. Salty teardrops poured from my tear ducts, but these tears were tears of closure, not pain. I felt all the years of disgust springing from my body like perspiration, and I knew February 10, 1996, would never haunt me again!

"Are you ready for your next adventure?" Othello asked as he brushed my hair away from my face.

"I'm ready to heal," I answered, "but I am also afraid of experiencing all of the situations that I've been running from! I am honestly scared of the person I used to be."

With a tone nothing more than a whisper, Othello sounded, "The only thing you have to fear is your eternity if you do not repair your soul."

Chapter *5*

My pitch-black surrounding began to lighten, and I realized Othello was no longer standing in front of me. As my atmosphere transformed once again, I found myself in the same position I once was on the hospital bed. Only now the bed I was lying on was my old dorm bed.

My dorm room was exactly the way I remembered. The window above my bed was even open, which was a common argument between my roommate Sarah and me. She favored air conditioning 24-7, which in the summer I didn't have a problem with, but on a beautiful fall day like today, it wasn't needed. I laughed out loud remembering all our petty disputes about "the window."

We both felt blessed having each other even if we did fight over stupid things sometimes. Sarah and I were like sisters; in fact, people often asked us if we were. We met a few weeks before school started, and we were so happy that we had so much in common. We shared similar looks, beliefs, and style. The only thing we disagreed on was men! I will get into that subject later. While our old high school friends were calling us with roommate horror stories, we were sharing our "things we would have never done without each other" stories. She was definitely becoming one of my best friends.

When I glanced out the window, I knew it was close to one of the holidays because the leaves were gold, fire-engine red, and orange. If I had to guess, it was probably right before Halloween. I didn't have to look at a calendar because my train of thought was interrupted by the slam of our door.

"Happy Halloween. Is that damn window open again?" Sarah sounded as she gleefully strolled in.

"It is beautiful out. We don't need the air, Ms. Freeze," I jokingly responded.

"Are you almost ready to leave?" she asked as she put away the groceries she picked up after class.

I had to think for a second, and then I remembered where we were going Halloween 1998. "The Smashing Pumpkins concert," I said out loud.

"What did you say, CeCe?" Sarah called from the small kitchen we had off our main room.

"Nothing," I said.

"You didn't forget about the concert?" she asked.

"Now how could I forget about the Smashing Pumpkins?" I said, astonished that she would even ask such a thing. The Smashing Pumpkins were one of my favorite bands, and the fact that they were playing on my favorite holiday was the absolute best!

"Baker's going to pick us up in fifteen minutes. Did you tell Thad that we were going?" Sarah summoned.

I responded with a sigh, "Yes, but I didn't tell him Baker was going."

Sarah didn't have to ask why. Thad wasn't fond of Baker, but then again, he didn't like any of my guy friends. He never had a reason; just the fact that they peed standing up was reason enough.

A demanding horn rang outside our window, and we dashed downstairs. As we entered the car, Baker asked a question that I thought was quite funny since I never even smoked weed.

"So, Ce, are you going to trip tonight?" asked Baker.

"Why is tonight any different than any other? I've never tripped before. And you better not be planning on it since you are driving," I demanded.

"Come on now," he said. "You know me strictly chronic. It's just Marcus is meeting us at the gate, and he got a couple green jellies. I just thought I'd ask to be polite."

Green jellies were the slang term for acid gel tabs. They came in almost all colors, kind of like M&M's. And just like M&M's, the green ones were supposed to be the best.

"I think we are going to stick strictly to drinking," Sarah interrupted confidently.

"Whatever tickles your tummy," Baker remarked. He always had jive comments, but he always made you laugh. Baker was your typical basketball type. His physique was tall and lanky. We shared the same major, and we had every single class together. We also were both Leos, so we were like cake and ice cream; we just went together. We bonded the first day of class, and our friendship was truly unique.

"So, Queen of Hearts, did you tell Thad you were planning on drinking tonight?"

Queen of Hearts was my nickname only Baker called me, and King of Spades was my own nickname for him. We started calling each other that after one of our infamous drinking poker games one night.

"Come on now. You know Thad would flip out and worry for no reason if I told him that. In fact, he doesn't even know you are the one taking us," I responded in a pissed-off manner because he asked a question he already knew the answer to.

Baker witnessed one of our biggest fights the first weekend of school because I did some Jell-O shots with some of my dorm buddies. The situation was totally innocent, but when I told Thad the next day, he flipped out and made me promise to never drink again, and I did because I loved him and didn't want him to worry. But then again, I just turned seventeen, and everyone knew freshman away at college often do what they want. So this was just the beginning of all the lies that I felt I had to tell Thad.

As we pulled into one of the parking lots, we could tell it was going to be a sold-out concert. I was so happy we bought our tickets months ago, because one of the ticket lines stretched about two football fields.

We cracked open Rolling Rocks as soon as we jumped out of the car.

"Where is Marcus meeting us?" I asked Baker.

"I told him to meet us before gate 8 around seven o'clock," he responded.

I had to wonder why Othello brought me back to this day. I mean, I remembered everything that happened that night, and yet I couldn't remember anything that could have damaged my soul, but I was happy to be back!

As we approached gate 8, we saw Marcus talking to some of his cronies.

"What's up, gang?" Marcus shouted.

"Are you ready to party?" I asked him as I finished my third beer.

"It looks like you started without me," Marcus added after he watched me trip on the way to throw away my beer bottle and practically fall into a garbage can.

I was always a two-can Sam. One beer to me was like four or five to most people. The gang just laughed as they gave me pointers on how not to look drunk as we walked past the security guards.

The band came on finally around ten, and by that time, I was seven beers and six shots of tequila to the wind! I was having a blast and was totally not in my right frame of mind when Marcus started to go on about the scenery.

"Those laser lights look like a million rainbows combined in one," Marcus replied in a fascinated tone.

Marcus had taken one of the green jellies about an hour prior, so the acid was just starting to hit him.

"I have never seen colors as bright and beautiful as I do right now," Marcus added.

Marcus was clearly in a state I had never seen him before. Marcus was like our dorm thug. He was always very high strung, kind of like one of that wind-up toys you had as a child; only he was wound too tight. But tonight he was mellow and relaxed, and I wondered if that little gel tab could make me as low-key as it made him.

"So do you feel strange at all?" I asked in a curious manner.

"Nope, I have never felt better," Marcus happily answered.

He held his hand out, and inside there was one of those miracle pills.

"Come into my world," he said with a devious smirk.

Without a second thought, all my reservations went out the door!

It wasn't till I popped the pill into my mouth that I realized I was trying to get into heaven, and here I was, ready to trip on acid. I had forgotten that I was simply reliving a memory, so I tried to bring the pill back up, and as I started gagging, Sarah ran over.

"CeCe, are you all right?" Sarah asked, panic stricken.

"I'm fine. I just took one of Marcus's pills without thinking," I said, very embarrassed.

"Don't worry, I'll take care of you," she said as she wrapped her arms around me.

It wasn't even a half hour later when I began to feel crippling sharp pains through my stomach. I ran to the bathroom to vomit, and Sarah followed. I threw up everything I ate that day, but I still didn't feel better.

Sarah thought if one of the guards saw me in this condition, I might get arrested, so she decided to sneak me out one of the back gates.

We both figured we'd meet up with everyone at the car. By the time we got back to the car, I was also having pains in my kidneys, and Sarah was afraid that if we waited for the boys, I would only get worse.

"I have to get you home and in bed," Sarah said as she picked her cell phone up and started dialing.

At this point, I was lying across the front of Baker's car, holding my stomach. I didn't feel like I was tripping, not that I knew what that felt like, but Marcus sure didn't look or feel like this. I started to worry, but my thoughts were interrupted when I heard Sarah yelling at this cab company on the phone.

"I don't care how much it costs! Send a cab here immediately," she hastily remarked to the stranger on the other line.

We were at the Starlight Amphitheater, which was about twenty miles from school, and I wondered how I was going to pay for this one as she hung up the phone.

"Sarah, how the hell are we going to pay for the cab?" I asked.

"Don't worry. I have seven hundred dollars in my dresser at home and will run up and get it while you wait in the cab," she answered in a nonchalant tone.

"I don't know how I am going to explain this one to my father when I ask him for the money to pay you back," I said in disbelief of the situation.

"You don't have to worry about paying me back," she muttered as the cab pulled in the crowded parking lot.

"How you doing, ladies?" the cab driver asked as we hopped in the car.

"We'll be fine once we're home," Sarah answered.

The car ride home was agony. I had to keep making the poor taxi driver pull over so I could vomit. After about a forty-minute drive, we arrived safely to our dorm.

"That'll be two hundred and seventy dollars, ladies," our cab driver happily muttered.

We knew we had totally just made his week.

"I have to run upstairs and get it, sir. I'll leave Cece with you as collateral," Sarah remarked as she hopped out the vehicle.

"What the hell do you two college girls do that you can afford a three-hundred-dollar cab ride?" our cab driver asked.

"We're waitresses," I said rudely, not liking what his tone was implying.

"Maybe I should go into waiting," the cabby added as Sarah opened the door and handed him three hundred and fifty dollars.

"Keep the change." She smiled as she helped me out of the car.

Chapter 6

Sarah practically carried me to our room, and as she was tucking me in bed, I started to wonder how she could have so easily afforded that cab ride. I mean, she came from a family of five. Her father died when she was very young, and her mother was still struggling to raise her three younger siblings. My thoughts were interrupted by the serious tone in her voice.

"I think it's time to tell you what I do, CeCe," she responded.

I lay in silence with my eyes barely open.

"I am a dancer," she then added.

My eyes shot open, and my mouth dropped to the floor. I mean, Sarah was definitely pretty enough to be a "dancer," but she wasn't the type of person whom you picture as being a stripper. She was beautiful and petite with a simple elegant class to her. She was also very health conscious and was in no way a druggie. And in college, she was the least promiscuous person I knew. Unfortunately, until now, I believed all the stereotypes about strippers. I thought all strippers were either on drugs or are in-the-closet prostitutes, but I could never think of Sarah that way! For the first time in my life, I realized that there was a whole world out there that I knew nothing about.

"Do you think less of me?" she asked in a curious tone.

"Sarah, I love you. What you do does not make you what you are," I reassured her. "I could never think less of you. I am just a little surprised," I answered.

"I am so glad you know. I hated hiding what I do from my best friend," Sarah remarked as she let out a sigh.

I totally forgot I was sick and had so many questions for her, but I didn't want to hound her. I actually found the conversation amusing because ever since I hit puberty, I was told that I should dance, but I never really gave it a second thought.

Sarah started to explain her situation. "I started dancing my senior year in high school to help my mom pay the bills and to help me build a nest egg so I could go to college. I watched my older sister get married to just get out of the house, and the only thing she gained was a controlling husband. I knew there was another way. Hey, I figure God gave me these looks for a reason, so I am going to use them," Sarah said proudly.

She then went on to tell me that she only danced topless, not fully nude, and she averaged a thousand dollars a week for only three shifts. She stressed that the men could in no way touch you, and if they did, they would be thrown out. Sarah made dancing seem like one big party, and I became more curious with each new sentence out of her mouth. I couldn't help but wonder what it would be like if I never had to return to my crummy job at Danzee's nightclub as a cocktail waitress. I could certainly give up getting drinks spilled on me.

"You know, CeCe, you have the body and the personality, if you're ever interested," Sarah exclaimed.

"I think Thad would kill me." I chuckled.

"Well, they are actually hiring waitresses right now. They wear shirts and tank tops, nothing too revealing. If you are interested, I can talk to Tony, my manager. And I know for a fact that they never make under one hundred and fifty a night."

"Now I could handle that," I muttered.

"Well," Sarah said, "I am going to go to bed, good night. Think about what I said."

As I lay in bed that night, I wasn't sure if I would wake up in the same bed. I was pretty sure Othello was pissed off that I drank and took acid. I actually was pretty scared because I thought I blew my chance to repair my soul. But as I began to drift asleep, I realized why he brought me back to this day. Maybe it wasn't to prevent me from doing my first heavy drug. Maybe it ran much deeper than that. Just maybe it was to show me how innocent I once was to all the things that only months later consumed and took over my life.

Chapter 7

To my very surprise, I awoke in my dorm room the next morning. I thought it was very strange that Othello didn't even appear in my dreams, but then again, maybe I wasn't through learning the lesson he was trying to teach me.

"Good morning, sleepy head," Sarah shouted as she flipped on the light switch in our main room. "I have an early class, so I am leaving now, but I want you to come to work with me tonight so you can apply for a waitressing job. Be ready around seven."

I barely had time to say okay before she slammed the door behind her. I was having second thoughts because I remembered exactly what happened the night I went with her, but I remembered what the only advice Othello gave me.

"Listen to your heart," Othello's voice echoed throughout the room. I was happy to hear from him because I now felt his presence again and knew he had been by my side the whole time.

Seven o'clock rolled around fast, and like clockwork, Sarah was home to pick me up. I was pretty quiet on the ride to work. Sarah kept asking if I was okay, and I tried to reassure her that I was, but I was secretly debating the whole idea.

"My boss is a little on the macho side, so don't mind him, but his gorgeous looks make up for his attitude," Sarah remarked as we entered the gentleman's club. It was funny to me that they called them gentleman's clubs when true gentlemen hardly hung out at places like that.

"Wow," I said as we walked through the lobby. I forgot how beautiful the club looked from the outside. I appreciated the beauty, kind of like a stranger would. Bare Elegance, the name of this particular club, was definitely one of the classiest joints, but no matter how fancy they decorated it, it was still a strip club!

Sarah and I took a seat in her manager Tony's office. As we waited for him, I looked around at all the pictures hanging on the walls of him degrading women, and I smiled knowing he was fired only a month later for in appropriate behavior. The nervousness I felt in the car went away, and I once again felt at home in a place that was so familiar yet so deceiving.

"What can I do you for?" shouted Tony as he entered the room. His comment was supposed to be funny, but Sarah and I just looked at each other and rolled our eyes as he sat down.

"I am here to apply for a cocktailing job," I sat confidently.

"You're joking, right?" Tony responded. "You are much to pretty to just cocktail. You should be dancing!"

I shot him a dumbfounded look and went on to tell him about my experience and was trying to give him references when he anxiously interrupted me.

"Look, you certainly are qualified, but I can't have prettier staff members than I have dancers, so if you want to dance, you can start tonight," he said in a hasty manner.

I was flattered that he thought I had what it took physically to dance, but his arrogant attitude got under my skin.

"I'm sorry for this inconvenience, sir, but I don't want to work for someone who thinks having ugly waitresses will make his dancers look better. I'll see you at home, Sarah," I said as I stood up and walked out of the office.

Tony rushed out of the office in an attempt to come after me, but it was too late. As I walked through the double doors that led to the main floor, I felt a sense of accomplishment. I was proud that I stuck up for myself, because I certainly didn't do that first time I was in his office. I couldn't help but laugh at myself when I thought about how cowardly I used to be.

The first time I met Tony, I explained that I was engaged and that I didn't think dancing was for me, but he made a deal with me that he knew he wouldn't lose. The deal was that I had to dance for two weeks, and if at the end of the two weeks I still didn't feel it was for me, then I could waitress. He knew for me it would be like hitting the lottery for millions and then settling for pennies. I mean, who honestly would be able give up that much money! Especially since two weeks was way too little time to really see the filth of the job. Tony smiled that day like the weasel he was, knowing it would be easier to kick a crack cocaine habit than to work around all that money and not be a part of it!

As I opened the doors to the main floor, I got another surprise. The customers that only minutes prior filled the rooms were gone, and I was once again standing clueless and alone in a pitch-black room.

Othello entered the club, greeting me with applause.

"You did it, child," he said with contentment in his voice. "I only wished you could have shown as much strength last night."

"About last night," I shyly responded.

"Let me tell you about last night," Othello interrupted. "You didn't do anything that damaged your soul. I am not condoning drug use, but at that stage in your life, it was experimental, and that's perfectly natural for teenagers. I don't expect you to change everything every time I bring you back to a memory, but knowing what to change is the reason for this journey. You were right about why I brought you back to last night, except you missed one thing."

"What was that?" I said in a curious tone.

Othello answered with a smile. "You were happy with yourself. Please try to remember that feeling, because you still have to weather many storms before you feel the warmth of the sunshine."

And with those words, he was gone again!

Chapter 8

As my surroundings transformed once again, I realized I was standing on a porch, and in front of me were the numbers 819. I took a few steps off the porch in disbelief. Here I was, back at the house Sarah and I rented after quitting college, but I was totally confused. If I told off Tony, the manager at Bare Elegance, then how could we afford this house? I didn't have to wait long for an answer.

"Well, don't just stand there, help me move this stuff in," Sarah said as she strolled up the walkway carrying boxes. "I think this is the smartest thing we've ever done. I mean, why should I stay in school when we don't even know what we want to do yet? Besides, we make more money than our professors."

I agreed with her as I grabbed a box from her arms and walked up the two flights of stairs to our living room. Our house was brick with white pillars. It reminded me of an old Southern plantation home. It used to be a five-bedroom, five-bath colonial, but when our landlords bought it, they decided to make it into a duplex. Sarah and I had the second floor of the house, which consisted of two bedrooms, two bathrooms, a dining room, a living room, a ranch kitchen, and an exercise room. It was also located on Grand Avenue in Mount Washington, a suburb of Pittsburgh, which overlooked the whole city. The view was absolutely breathtaking, but also was the price.

As I walked into our living room, floods of memories rushed into my head. I froze like a stiff, practically dropping the box I was carrying.

"What's wrong, CeCe? You look like you've seen a ghost," committed Sarah.

I thought to myself, if only she knew! The house looked exactly how I remembered. Oatmeal-color Berber carpet stretched through the living areas, and porcelain tile accented the kitchen and bathrooms. Beautiful cherrywood floors were refinished and nicely buffed in both the bedrooms. All the rooms were freshly painted antique white, with cream-colored crown molding adorning the ceiling and baseboards. The house was uniquely modern yet classic at the same time. Everything about the house felt clean and familiar.

That night we got all our things moved in, and as we were lying on the couch, the conversation turned to work.

"You know, I am surprised that you stood up to Tony," Sarah began. "He complimented me on having you for a friend, and also said that you had a character charm he would have never let get away."

Turns out even after telling him off, I still became a dancer. I just never dealt with the sexual harassment I dealt with the first time around!

"Hey, Sarah, what's the date today?" I asked.

"What do you mean what's the date? We just signed and dated the lease ten minutes ago. Besides, how could you forget you have your first date with Mario?" Sarah said.

And once again I didn't need to look at a calendar. I knew it was April 5, 1999, another day I had hid in the depth of my soul. At this point in my life, I had been dancing for six months. It was also nearly that long since I had broken up with Thad. Tonight was my first date with someone new in almost five years, but with just the mention of Mario's name, my palms began to sweat.

Mario was an extremely charming thirty-one-year-old, with coal-black hair, sky-blue eyes, and beautiful olive skin. He was what we call in a strip club a regular. Mario was a private investigator who worked for the Pittsburgh Police Department. He and his detective buddies would come in every Wednesday night, and to my untrained eye, he seemed like a perfect gentleman. For the last four months, he had come in weekly and hounded me for my number, but I never surrendered. I think deep inside I knew he was trouble, but one night after many glasses of pinot noir, I let his piercing eyes penetrate my fragile heart, and I gave in! Besides the fact that I met him in a strip club, he seemed like the perfect guy. He was a distinguished member of society who grew up in an Italian Catholic family, and he was a detective for the city! I had nothing to worry about, right? That question would haunt me the rest of my life!

My whole body began to feel numb as flashbacks hit me like waves crashing on the beach. I suddenly realized that if I had listened to my heart, I would've never agreed to going out with Mario, but before I could pick up the phone to cancel, I found myself sitting in Mario's Ford

Explorer. I guess changing this life experience was not going to be as easy as my decisions before!

As I sat across him, it took all my strength not to punch him in the face. "What's that look for, CeCe?" Mario replied questionably. I wanted to tell him it was a look of disgust for all the pain and mistrust he would never have to deal with, and for all the hearts I would break because of him, but almost silently, I replied, "No reason."

The night was unnervingly chilly, which must have been foreshadowing what was about to happen! I stared in disbelief out the window when I realized he was driving in the opposite direction of the way back to my house. "Where are we going?" I asked.

"It's a surprise!" he playfully exclaimed.

"I don't like surprises," I said sternly.

"Will you relax, CeCe? I just want you to meet my roommate before I take you home."

As we pulled into the driveway, I didn't notice any other cars, but I figured his room-mate's car was probably in the garage.

"He must not be home," Mario remarked.

That very line sent memories of terror through my heart. Floods of memories poured through my mind, and I didn't understand what was going on. I told him I wanted to go home, so why wasn't this life lesson over? Was I really supposed to relive the most violent night of my life?

My hands started to shake, and I pondered jumping out of the car. I felt like the helpless teenager I once was, and tears began to form in my eyes.

As Mario parked the car, I prayed Othello was watching over me. I knew he was the only one that could protect me from the monster that lay behind Mario's beautiful blue eyes. "Are you going to get out of the car?" Mario asked. His words jolted me out of the past into the very pressing present. I was holding on to the seat with a death grip.

"Yeah, I guess I have to," I softly spoke.

"Would you like something to drink?" he replied.

"No, I am fine. I have a long day ahead of me tomorrow," I said hastily.

"Well, come inside so I can grab a sweatshirt. It's cold out here." His voice was deceiving like he cared.

"Not as cold as your heart," I spoke underneath my breath.

As I walked up the creaky stairs to his house, my stomach began to turn, for I knew what was about to happen, but there was nothing I could do to stop it.

We were only a few steps inside the house when I felt one of his arms grab my wrists and lock them together behind my back, while the other arm he wrapped around my neck. I froze in shock just like the last time. He lifted me off the floor and held me in a chokehold. As I started to lose consciousness, he released his grip around my neck. He clearly wanted me to remember this. I heard Othello in the back of my mind whisper, "Fight, like you've never fought before." As Mario tried to pull down my jeans with his one free arm, I encountered a strength I never knew I had, but the harder I tried to fight, the angrier he got. I kicked, I screamed, I tried to struggle, but there was nothing I could do to escape from his 220-pound grip. My body grew numb as he entered my womb, and with each of his pelvic thrusts, I retreated to a place in my head where I could feel no pain. He threw my body around like a weathered old rag doll. From position to position, he somehow knew how to keep my arms locked behind me, a tactic every cop probably knew. My head bounced off one of his end tables, and just as I began to feel the blood rush from my temple into my eardrum, I was pulled like a jolt of lightning from my body.

Chapter 9

I was falling once again, but I didn't care where to. At this point, I contemplated giving up on repairing my soul. The rape seemed to be worse the second time around, and I couldn't possibly understand why I had to experience it again.

My body came to a screeching halt on what felt like a bed of feathers. When I opened my eyes, I realized I was lying safe and sound in my bedroom, but that did nothing to comfort me. Dead silence fell all around the room. The only sound audible was my tears hitting the polished wood underneath my feet. My body was limp with exhaustion, and when I closed my eyes, I prayed not to wake up.

The next morning, Sarah cheerfully walked into my room.

"I didn't hear you come home last night. You must have had a good night," she unknowingly claimed.

I lay in disarray, clenching my head in my aching hands, not responding to her question.

"Are you all right, CeCe?" Sarah asked as she began to shake me.

I was curled up in the corner of my bed, numb from the night before. As I rolled over on to my back, Sarah gasped and put her arms over her mouth.

"What the hell happened to your face?" she asked petrified with fear.

"Mario," I said, desperately choking down the tears.

"What?" she sounded off, just as surprised as I was about the situation.

She crawled in bed with me and examined my entire body. She began counting out loud all the marks Mario had left. I had sixteen bruises ranging from head to toe.

"I will be right back," Sarah remarked as she rolled out of bed.

She walked back into my room, holding a disposable camera.

As she started taking pictures, I threw my hands over my face and asked her to stop. The flash from the camera was hurting my swollen eyes.

"No, I cannot stop, we need pictures for proof," she replied.

"Proof for what?" I asked angrily.

"The police," she remarked, astonished I even asked.

"The police." I chuckled. "Don't you get it? He is the police!"

A wave of disbelief washed over both of us, and all she could do to comfort me was hold me. There were no words to ease my teetered soul. I had been tortured from the one source that vowed to serve and protect. She knew as much as I did a cop's word over a "stripper" would always prevail.

As I lay in the warmth of Sarah's arms, I felt Othello's presence draw near. In a blink of an eye, Sarah was gone again, and Othello was the one cradling me in his arms.

"I am so sorry you had to relive that experience," he said sadly.

"I feel paralyzed again," I responded.

"I brought you back there because that day was the last time you fought for your life. That was the last time you showed you wanted to live.

After the rape, you didn't care what happened to you, or what you did to anyone else. I wish I could have avoided bringing you back to that memory, but reliving that day is very crucial to the survival of this mission," Othello calmly explained.

"I don't feel any different than I did six years ago. What was I supposed to learn from that?" I asked in a monotone voice.

"What you learned," Othello begun, "you already expressed in your head when you were walking up the path to Mario's house. There was nothing you could've done. The rape wasn't your fault, and there was no way to prevent it. I wish that experience wasn't written into your chart, but for a reason that has not been revealed yet, it is part of your journey! You know the saying 'Bad things happen to good people.'"

"Yes," I remarked curiously.

"Well, sometimes bad things happen to good people, because those good people can the turn negative things that happen to them into positive things, not only for them, but for thousands of people! You were a person that God blessed with many talents, and one of those talents was your unique communication skills. People always felt uncensored around you. CeCe, you had such an overwhelming presence that when you spoke, people actually listened. You were the perfect advocate. You have the ability to help women understand rape is never a women's fault."

"I never thought any positive could ever come out of that horrific day," I remarked, "but you are right. I always loved helping other people. I was always the friend to turn to for comfort or consoling. I got so much satisfaction knowing I could help heal, and in turn, I guess I would have been healing myself if I would have spoken out."

"I think you are finally starting to get it," Othello began. "Maybe you wouldn't've been able to put Mario away for his crime, but you would have been able to look at yourself in the mirror without the shame of his doing. Trust me, child, God will deal with dark energies such as himself. Dark entities do not get a chance to repair their souls."

Othello's words brought a peace of mind I never knew existed. I felt an innocence I hadn't known since I was a child. I no longer wished I never would have met Mario; I only wished I would've become a fighter instead of a victim. I also no longer wished he was lying facedown in the Hudson River. I only prayed he got help so he could no longer hurt anyone else.

Chapter *10*

Fighting back would seem to be the motto for my next mission also. I had woken up from one nightmare to another. I could feel my backbones digging into my bedroom floor. I was incoherent and barely breathing. I rolled over to look at my alarm clock, and it read 1:11. I wasn't sure, due to the fact that my blinds were closed, whether it was night or day. As I rose to my feet, I caught a glimpse of myself in the mirror and almost fainted. For the first time in my life, I was seeing myself as anorexic and frail. My once-vibrant almond eyes were sunken in and surrounded by giant black circles. My collarbones poked through my skin like a skeleton, and my once-plump chest looked concaved. I quickly turned around and yanked at the back of my jeans so I could read the tag. My mouth dropped as I read size double 0. I remembered being a 0 and seeing myself as a 10. For the first time in my life, I was really seeing myself. My eyes were open to what the rest of the world saw, and I now understood why people who knew me my whole life stared in disbelief every time they saw me. I had wasted away to bare bones.

The reason for it was just as disheartening, and it lay scattered on my nightstand along with a swizzle straw. After the rape, I succumbed to any temptation that numbed my mind from the horrible memories, even if it was only a part-time fix.

I never snorted cocaine with money because I thought it was bad luck. It is pretty funny how a drug addict could blame any unfortunate episode on anything but the drug itself. I examined my body with disbelief. See, what was different about me was I was a coke addict who hated the drug. All users say they hate the drug when they are crashing, but I never even enjoyed the high. Cocaine only masked a much bigger problem I had been dealing with all my life, a severe eating disorder, accompanied by obsessive body image disorder. The thinner I would get, the fatter the reflection was staring back at me. I had always seen food as the enemy, and by doing cocaine, I was never hungry, and I was the skinniest I had ever been. It also let my mind drift from all the shame I knew as my life. In my distorted mind, a double plus. It wasn't until I decided to break up with my drug dealer boyfriend that I realized I even had a problem. A fifteen-hundred-a-week problem! I no longer controlled anything about myself; the drug controlled me. The pretentious powder dictated everything in my life. I felt I couldn't do anything without it! I would do a line when I woke up and while I was at the gym, the tanning salon, the grocery store, even to just sit and do my monthly bills.

I knew right away. Othello brought me back to see how incredibly disastrous my outlook on life was and how obsessed with physical appearance I once was. I was willing to lie awake days at a time just to be thin—line after line, night after night. I was slowly killing myself even back then!

I fought the temptation to snort a line as I walked past my dresser. I opened my bedroom door and walked down my empty hallway that led to Sarah's room.

"Knock, knock," I said as I slowly opened her bedroom door.

As the door swung open, my heart broke. The room was as empty as my sinful soul. Her beautiful sleigh bed was gone, but the indents from it were still fresh in the carpet. The only thing left in the room was a peach envelope sitting on her window panel. It was the perfect place to leave her good-bye. I was sad to realize the window was something we would never fight over again.

I stood in disbelief in the fact that she was gone. Sara had been my world for the last two years. My whole outlook on life had changed, whether good or bad, because of her. She was much more than my roommate in college; she was my mentor.

Leaving her final words on the windowpane made me want to laugh yet break into tears at the same time.

I walked over and opened the letter. I never knew opening it would be like opening Pandora's box. As I started to read the letter, tears welled in my eyes.

The opening statement read, "CeCe, my one innocent love, you taught me life isn't about money or appearances; it is about making your dreams a reality. Because of you, I know there are still real people left in the world. I will never forget your innocent soul. Never lose the naïveté I always bitched about, and forgive me for leaving you. I hope you come see me in Vegas—Sarah."

I was overwhelmed with insecurity and peace. For the last two years, Sarah and I were like sisters, best friends, coworkers, roommates, and in an unlikely, unexplainable way, soul mates. She had taught me how to make money in our business by playing the game. We were simply actresses playing out a fantasy. Men only spent money on us because of the severe delusion that their fantasies would one day become a reality. You had to be cunning in our world. Besides, if men knew they never had a chance, the cats wouldn't come out to chase.

Sarah had taught me to expect the very least and the very worst from men, so I had no high expectations when it came to the opposite sex, but I never expected a woman to cause me the most excoriating heartache I had ever known. Her leaving felt like being buried alive and only she held the shovel that could dig me free. And almost as fast as she was gone, I snapped back to reality: I had a life to lead, and I wanted it to be meaningful with or without her.

I picked myself off the floor and dragged myself back to the temptation that lay on my dresser. It was clear what I had to do. I had to get rid of everything in my life that was killing me, and cocaine was my number 1 enemy. I grabbed a deck of playing cards and pulled the first card on the top. I didn't think it was a coincidence it was the Queen of Hearts. I let out a sigh and shook my head as I scraped the excess lines back into my secret stash. Nearly an ounce of cocaine lay in the palms of my hands, and I knew just what to do with it. Most people would have sold it or flushed it, but I knew the easier for me to get rid of it meant the easier it would be for it to get ahold of me again.

I called all my so-called druggie friends to come over. It was sad that at that point in my life I didn't associate with anyone that wouldn't turn down free drugs no matter what time it was. Within an hour, eight cronies sat in a circle around my dining room table, still awake from the night before. I sat there watching all of them sniff their reality into oblivion. And as my stash dwindled away, I felt the ties that bound me to the drug loosen. I knew as long as I was in a shady profession, I would have to be around it, and I needed to have the strength not to be corrupted. My body began to sweat as the last line lay in perfect parallel to my face. I have to admit, it took all my courage not to be the one to do it, but I resisted, and with a simple no, I grew one step closer to taking back my soul and my life!

Chapter *11*

I left the table alone, leaving all my friends behind, but as I turned the hallway, I noticed out of the corner of my eye my dining room table was empty. I opened the creaky door to my bedroom, and there sat Othello on my bed.

"You did very good, my child," he responded.

"It honestly wasn't that hard," I answered. "I hated that drug. I only wished I could've seen myself then."

"Life is always easier in hindsight," Othello's words always had such a warming truth to them.

"I just wanted to let you know you might not see me for a while. I have given you guidance. Now you must stand on your own." Othello's coal-black eyes pierced right through me. "I have faith in you. Now you must have faith in yourself. You know right from wrong, and if all goes well, I will see you on the other side," he reassured.

Othello's appearance faded before I could respond or even thank him. An uncanny fear washed over me, for I had no clue what was about to happen. All I knew was I was alone, but I was ready for my next adventure because I had earned a respect for myself I never had before. So I walked around my apartment, studying every inch. When I came to Sarah's room, I placed one hand on the doorknob and the other on the deadbolt. I knew I was not only closing her door; I was closing a chapter to my life!

I walked down the spiral staircase to our garage, and with only a suitcase in my hand, I got in my car and drove away. I watched my house get smaller and smaller in the distance until only the lights at the top of Mount Washington were visible. At first I wasn't sure where I was driving to, but a tiny voice in my head whispered it was time to go home, my real home. I hadn't been home in months even though I only lived forty-five minutes away. I had been avoiding my parents for many reasons, but the shame of my job and the influences it had on me were the main reasons.

I was never one to speed, but my right foot felt as heavy as lead as I whipped around the back roads toward my old country town. Like a slap in the face, I realized cocaine also isolated me from my family. I was too embarrassed to let anyone know I was an addict, so I completely ignored everyone who meant the world to me. I was never in such a hurry to get home. I went running from my small town at seventeen for the bright lights of the city, and now I felt myself driving faster than ever to get back.

As I pulled in my mother's driveway, I realized it was the middle of the night, and I didn't have a key. I was scared my alcoholic stepfather would flip out on my mother, so I debated knocking on the door. It took me nearly fifteen minutes to get up the courage to walk up her steps. I tried to knock softly, but there was no answer, so I decided I had to ring the doorbell. My mother turned on the porch light and cracked the door. Her squinty eyes quickly opened with joy when she realized it was me.

"CeCe!" She hugged me. "What, how— never mind. I am just glad you are okay and that you are home."

It had been so long since I let anyone besides Sarah comfort me; it felt almost foreign. It had probably been almost three years since I let it come from my mother.

The look in my mother's eyes was so sad. As she made me green tea, my favorite, I noticed she was avoiding looking at my body. I knew it was absolutely killing her not to say something about my emaciated frame. To say I was confrontational would be a desperate understatement, but in the last year, the drugs made me worse. My mother, on the other hand, was very sweet and docile and would do anything to avoid an argument, so I knew it was up to me to speak up first.

"I need help, Mom." I sobbed and threw my hands over my face.

"Are you not eating again?" she asked.

"Yes, but not for the reason you are thinking." I nodded as I spoke. I almost choked on the words, but I knew my ghost would forever haunt me if I didn't let it out of the closet. I had been living a lie for so long it was finally time to tell the truth.

My mom's eyes were such a beautiful innocent blue. I almost wished I could build a boat and sail away in their calming waters. It broke my heart that I was about to cause a hurricane in them.

"I have been doing a lot of things I am not proud of, Mom," I said shamelessly.

Silence fell over the kitchen, and I felt like an elephant was sitting on my vocal cords. She stared so caringly. I hated myself once again for having to hurt her.

"It's cocaine," I expelled.

"It will be okay. We will do whatever we have to," my mother gently responded.

There were no questions, no disappointing statements, just the warmth of a mother's touch, and maybe all along that was all I needed.

She got the winter blankets out of the linen closet and made up the couch for me. It felt so good to be taken care of. I had been so ashamed to come home, but home was the most comforting place. My mom kissed my forehead and tucked me in just like she did when I was five. I lay on the couch, staring at all the pictures on the wall of my brothers and me. I drifted to sleep, wanting to wake up the little girl on the wall again.

Chapter 12

"Wake up, angel," my mother said as she gently tugged at my shoulder. "I am making blueberry pancakes. I need to put some weight on you," she jokingly remarked.

I stretched my arms into the sweet-smelling air as I stood from the lumpy couch. I quickly sat back down when I felt so dizzy I could have passed out. I knew it was from lack of nutrition. It had probably been at least two days since I ate an actual meal.

I stumbled into the kitchen and was overwhelmed with the amazing aroma of Bisquick.

"I hope you do not mind. I took the liberty of calling Dr. Summers this morning to make an appointment for you," my mom said.

"Dr. Summers, Mom?" I asked, shocked.

Dr. Summers had been my doctor since I was three years old. The most serious problem she had seen from me was a black eye from soccer when I was in ninth grade. Cocaine was a very taboo issue in my small town, period, let alone from a former cheerleader and just two years earlier was an honor student, but I was in no position to argue. I knew it was time to let my mother actually be a mother.

After breakfast my mom helped me get dressed, and we headed for the doctor's office. As we walked through the doorway, I was surprised to see the office seemed practically timeless. Highlight magazines and Curious George books were still left scattered on the counters, and circus-themed border still adorned the walls. I thought it was funny how hundreds of people had passed through this room, and it remained virtually untouched; however, only a few years had passed through me, yet I remained practically unrecognizable.

My doctor's assistant, Peggy, had been with Dr. Summers's since I was in middle school, and her eyes opened in awe with only one look at me. Only because of my mother's presence did she even know who I was. As she called me back to get weighed, she tried not to stare, but her wondrous horror shone right through.

I stepped onto the old-fashioned manual scale. As she pushed the iron weight back, even my eyes grew in disbelief. "Just shy of one hundred," Peggy quietly remarked as she slid the scale back. "I am going to ask your mother to come back while Dr. Summers's examines you. Is that okay?"

"That is fine," I answered back. And that was the only thing that was fine about the whole situation.

My mother was too scared to ask what I weighed, so we ignored the subject completely. I sat anxiously awaiting Dr. Summers's presence, on the vinyl examining chair; I was so ashamed of my state of mind, the condition of my body, and the awful secrets that lay behind both.

As my mind raced with all the possible questions I would have to answer, the door swung open, and Dr. Summers's beautiful smile quieted the haunting.

"How are you, sweetie?" she asked in a very friendly manner.

"I have seen better days," I sadly exclaimed.

"Haven't we all," she quickly responded.

I think she was trying to ease the tension of a very stressful room.

Dr. Summers sat on her rolling chair and pulled the chair up between my knees, just like she used to do when I was a child.

"So do you want to tell me how you lost nearly thirty-three pounds since I have seen you last?" As she glanced down at her chart, her head quickly jerked up, and her eyes peered at mine almost as if we were in a dwelling match. "Only nine months ago?" Her question was like a posing cat ready to pounce and catch its prey.

My eyes hastily turned to the floor, and the dreaded answer came out of my mouth. "I have been using cocaine for about five months."

"Is that all?" Dr. Summers asked in a nonchalant way.

"No." My eyes met hers once again, and my mom's eyes pried open. "I have also been doing a little ecstasy on occasion," I said as my head dropped once again.

Both my mother and Dr. Summers let out a sigh of disgust. Then Dr. Summers replied, "I am not too familiar with that drug, so you have to give me a day to do some research on treatment for that drug, but the cocaine is a serious problem. There are a few medications I can prescribe to help with the withdrawals—"

I interrupted promptly, "No medication. I want to do this cold turkey."

"Honey," Dr. Summer's started, "I wish you had the strength too, but I don't think you do."

"I know I do. I made this decision, knowing I have to get through life without any crutches," I said harshly.

"Well, you are an adult, CeCe, so I cannot force you, but I know the statistics of people returning to the drugs," she said doubtfully.

"So do I, Dr. Summers," I said sternly. "I not only know the statistics. I know the demons behind the drug, and I have faced mine already. I've got a glimpse into my future if I continue on this path, and that is the only sedative I need."

She knew I was determined to at least try this on my own, so she quickly changed the subject.

"Well, have you had any other changes, besides weight loss?"

I quickly answered, "I have been vomiting a lot after meals, but I figured it was because my stomach has shrunk so much from the lack of food, and I frequently have a pain in the middle upper part of my stomach that comes on strongly after I eat as well."

"Well," Dr. Summer's began, "you might have a few ulcers or acid reflux. It's probably not anything serious, but we'll check it out anyways. I want you to head over to the hospital after we are through, and we will run some tests."

The visit wasn't as excoriating as I anticipated, but it was heartbreaking for my mother to see her once-beautiful angel looked upon as an addict.

As we drove over to the hospital for further tests, my mother thought it was a good idea to call my father and let him know what was going on. I instantly became numb. I was always my father's little princess, and tears welled in my eyes, knowing I was going to slay his fairy tale.

I waited for the on-call doctor to call my name as my mom went outside to call my father on her cell phone.

I was already back in examining room number 6, before my father and stepmother arrived at the hospital. I was not sure how my mother was even going to explain what was going on.

As my mind raced from lie to lie to explain any other reason for my rapid weight loss, and the horrible ingestion, the cloth curtain swung open, and the on-call doctor quickly introduced himself. I was so relieved I didn't know him, and better yet, he had no distorted memory of who I was.

"Hi, I am Dr. Ryan. I see Dr. Summers has ordered some routine tests to check for your tummy troubles." His face was friendly, and he looked very young, probably a first-year resident, and acted as if he had no clue to my shameful secret.

As he wheeled me to an observation room, I could hear my mom and dad screaming at each other from the other side of the hospital. A feeling of guilt turned my already-sour stomach upside down. My parents never needed a reason to fight; it just came natural, so I felt like the most horrible child.

Dr. Ryan prepped me in front of a huge X-ray machine and told me to chug this chalky liquid as fast as I could. The milk of magnesia–tasting fluid almost came up as fast as it went down. As I forced myself not to vomit, Dr. Ryan yelled out, "Just hold it down, a few more minutes, CeCe."

Two minutes felt like two years as the chunky milkshake twisted like summersaults inside my tummy.

As soon as the words "We are finished" popped out of his mouth, all the horrid liquid came out of mine. I vomited everything that was in my stomach into the nearby trashcan.

"I am sorry. I know that stuff is rancid, but it is crucial," Dr. Ryan said with much sympathy. "Just lie back on that gurney. We should have results shortly."

I lay in silence, quite frankly disbelieving what I had done to myself. I was nineteen, scared, and pondering the gruesome truth about what I might have done to my insides.

What happened next seemed like a scene out of a mental hospital. Four doctors I had not seen prior rushed into the room, and as I lay in disarray, each one circled around me. I could still hear my dad's voice stifling down the hallway.

"We are only doing this for your protection, CeCe," one doctor said, and within seconds, two body straps were wrapped over my shoulders and under my knees.

"What the hell is going on?" I said hysterically as I panicked, trying to free myself from the strangling seatbelts.

Apparently, the doctor went out and told my parents that my gallbladder had approximately thirty-six tiny holes in it and was only functioning at 9 percent. My kidneys and liver also looked damaged, and his only explanation for this was severe alcoholism, but most likely given my age, heroin.

My father rose to his feet and suspiciously replied, "No way, she is an honor student. There is no way she is using heroin. This is a child that never even smoked weed."

"Well," Mr. DeMarco said, "ninety-nine percent of the time, we only see organs damaged like this in those situations."

My father's suspicions turned to rage and ordered them to restrain me while they checked every inch of my body for possible needle marks.

The doctors argued first with my father's requests but caved due to reasons I am still not sure of.

As the doctors scanned every inch of my body, they told me what they were searching for. At first I put up a fight, but when I realized I had nothing to hide, I gave up. I had never, even in my most fucked-up state, even thought about putting a needle into any part of my body. I thought of heroin addicts as scum and was so disgusted to find out later that the high, or the roll, you get from ecstasy was from no other than the disgusting drug itself.

The doctors seemed pleased to go out and tell my family I had no visible signs of needles or prior tracks, but they were puzzled to the severe damage only a few pills caused. I was soon to become one of the youngest kids in Pennsylvania to have my gallbladder removed.

They wheeled me to the third floor and set my surgery for 7:00 a.m. All my family had left the hospital, and I was there once again alone. I lay in pain, staring at a faded yellow wall for what felt like an eternity.

"Knock, knock," I heard from a familiar voice.

I turned in disbelief and saw Thad standing there with two gardenias.

"How are you feeling, sweetie?"

"How do I look?" I said in a nonchalant way.

He didn't have to say anything; I knew my physical presence was as shocking to him as it was to me.

"Who told you I was home?" I casually asked.

"Come on, CeCe. You have been home for eight hours. All of the 1,800 people in this town know by now."

I laughed and nodded, knowing he was probably speaking the truth.

"You wanna tell me what is going on, CeCe?"

I pushed my thinning hair back from my face and replied, "I don't want to break your heart more than I already have."

"Losing you was the worst thing that ever happened to me, but seeing that somewhere along the way you have lost yourself is more painful than any words."

"Just hold me," I started to say when I felt his comforting embrace encircle my tiny frame.

We lay in utter silence for the next hour, but our souls were recapping like old fools. I knew he was disappointed in me, but I never felt it. He was the one person who knew how incredibly fragile my inner core truly was.

"Excuse me, visiting hours is over."

A nurse said with a soft tone as she cracked open my hospital room door and peeked in.

"I guess that is my clue to leave," Thad said as he pulled from my desperate embrace.

"I'll stop by tomorrow to check on you after surgery, if you would like."

"I would love that," I said as I flashed the devious smile that he once adored.

With a soft kiss, he slipped out of the room as gently as he entered. I lay in silence, wondering if that would be the last time I would ever stare in his chocolate eyes or feel his calming words radiate like beams of light through my soul. I folded my hands and prayed to Othello that if Thad and I couldn't find ourselves back to each other, that he would meet a woman that loved him ten times more than my selfish nature ever could. And on a prayer, I fell deep asleep with only memories of happier times.

I partially awoke to two doctors standing over me and tried to make out their words, but all I could comprehend was mumbling. I became aware that my right arm was slowly becoming numb. I looked down to see why and felt my conscious mind fade to oblivion. And as if nothing happened, I awoke to a blissful fog.

At first I thought I was dreaming, and then I realized I was once again floating over my lifeless body. A three-inch-thick plastic tube was placed over my mouth, and it ran down inside my throat. Medical tape was stretched over my eyes. My golden hair was hiding underneath a cap, and what showed of my skin looked almost pale. The room was fairly quiet except for the persistent bleeps from my heart monitor. I watched one surgeon play with his instruments almost as if he would chopsticks, while another marked my stomach with a purple pen. With one steady movement, the one doctor put the knife to my skin and made an incision in my upper abdominal wall. I felt myself gasp and gripped my side. I was invisible to the doctors above, but my soul was still very connected to my body. I felt the next two cuts they made, but the pain was not what bothered me. I realized from a distance the disrespect I once had for my own beautiful body, and it began to overwhelm me. I watched skilled professionals carefully cut and sew my body and show it more consideration than I ever did.

Then within a split second, the peaceful room turned to chaos. My heart monitor went from a rhythmic harmony to a persistent alarm. The two calm surgeons looked at each other with confusion and distress.

"Shock her now," the one doctor demanded. "We're losing her."

I panicked and started screaming at the top of my lungs.

"Othello, Othello, what the hell is happening?"

My eager eyes scanned the room with discretion, but Othello was nowhere to be found. I tried to push myself back toward my body, but I had no strength. The three feet between myself and my body felt like a football field.

A flood of doctors rushed into the room, while one nurse pressed the electric handles to my lifeless chest.

With one jolt my body rose up from the bed, and my monitor began to climb back to its previous pace.

I took a deep breath and a sigh of relief, and as I exhaled, I felt my soul being pulled like I was in a windpipe back into my body. My eyes broke free from the restraining tape and opened with a completely new outlook on life and death.

"You gave us quite a scare," my surgeon said as he pulled the paper mask away from his face.

I gasped and let out a sigh of relief as I realized who the familiar face was from beyond the mask. It was my old friend Othello, and he had been there all along.

Chapter *13*

Othello snapped the mask back to his face, and his presence began to disappear into the blinding bright lights of my operating room. I had no time to ask where or when I would see him again. The yellow-colored lights grew brighter and brighter until they turned unbearable. The glare was so intense I felt as I was staring directly into raw sunlight. I raised my forearms above my face to shield me from the dramatic gleams. As I crossed my arms together, I felt another strange sensation, but it was different from the pain I felt while I watched the surgeons slice me. My elbows began to burn almost as if I were standing too close to an open flame. I partially opened my eyes to see if I could see where this new sensation was coming from. Glistening lights radiated from my skin, and gold beams seemed to stream from every chakra of my body. I felt an unexplainable release as all the tubes, IV, and medical tape fell in slow motion from my body.

The gold beams encircled my whole being and bonded together to form a circle of liquid gold slowly flowing freely around me. The gold ball grew brighter and warmer as it moved in an everlasting circle of energy entrapping me. As the ball spun faster, it gently lifted me from the cold gurney up into its hot core. I remained dead still in the center of the circle while the golden ball picked up speed and began to move vertically. I was floating freely, completely rejuvenated, in a circle of energetic love. The energy from the ball began to fill up my entire space, sending rays of positive exhilaration down my spine.

I closed my eyes and inhaled the beautiful life that encompassed my soul. The golden ball was on its own path and had its own destination, but I had no clue why it had chosen me to accompany it for the ride. I just bathed in the warmth and love until my ball started to break down as fast as it appeared.

The liquid gold ball circling me began to lose its heat and speed. It slowly started to lose its rhythm and color, and like a balloon that had been stretched too far, it popped. Millions of gold particles exploded into the air, and I was released from its womb. I started to free-fall but quickly landed on what felt like a fisherman's net.

I opened my eyes once again to see flashes of light, but these were not the same warm lights as before. The flashing lights were loud and ear-piercing. They were cold and uncomfortable, and I felt like someone was hitting my head with a hammer every time they went off. I rolled to my side and realized I was lying in a hammock with nothing covering me but a few strands of fake seaweed.

I casually glanced down to see myself, and my whole body had changed. I was no longer frail. My image was dramatically distorted into a picture-perfect Barbie doll. Plastic vines covered the outside while plastic bags filled my once-sunken chest. Every muscle in my body was defined, and fake black wavy hair dangled down my curvy voluptuous hips.

I sat up and placed my sculpted legs onto the cement floor beneath me.

"CeCe, we are not done with you yet!" a man's voice yelled from above.

The man was Paige Henson, a young hot-shot photographer who was more impressed with his pictures than anyone else was. He had

Bette Davis blue eyes and balding brown hair. He talked with a New Jersey accent but tried to pass it off as New York. I was introduced to him by a coworker whom he represented. At first I thought he was a sleaze, but I thought any money I could make outside of that club was a good idea. It never dawned on me that I was still selling a part of my soul.

"Can I take a break, Paige?" I smugly asked.

"Come on, CeCe, you know time is money, and I only have the studio booked for another half hour."

"I need a break," I demanded in a more brass tone.

"All right, doll face. You can take five."

Paige acted a lot tougher than he actually was. He knew better than to talk back to me because I was his one model that would walk off a set and not think twice about the consequences.

I grabbed a bath towel that lay crumbled next to the hammock, wrapped it around my toned torso, and headed for the dressing room. As I opened the door, I caught a glimpse of myself in the full-length mirror. I dropped my towel and stared in amazement at some surgeon's creation. I ran my fingers along my lightly scarred nipples and traced my mouth with the other. I had been blessed with full lips from birth, but they had definitely been enhanced. I then ran my fingers through my hair and felt seams. Yep, that was fake too! My skin was also three shades darker than the beautiful olive complexion I once had, and my envious green eyes were covered with brown contacts, and all I could feel was sadness when I realized what extremes I had gone too to be someone's image of perfect. Who was this person looking back at me, and what did all these outside fixes do to my inside?

And it hit me like a ton of bricks; I was wearing a mask. The more money, time, and attention I gave to physically please myself, the more exhausted and disgusted I got from the result, because nothing fake was ever truly me. I had spent years running, and this was the time to address the real issues. Each time I felt insecure, I fixed a body part that wasn't the culprit. All along the only body part that needed fixed was my heart! In a moment of pure insanity, I was about to grab scissors off the vanity, when my dressing room door opened, and there stood Paige with Ken Nelson, the owner of the studio.

"Excuse me," I said as I pushed the door back in both of their faces.

Ken caught the door with his right forearm. His looks fit the typical Scottsdale artificial businessman. He was a trust fund baby who never had to work a day in his life. He valued nothing in life but his Mercedes AMG. His hair was coal black with a touch of gray at his ear lobes, and his deep-set blue eyes were always bloodshot from his diet of cocaine and alcohol.

I was not one of his girls, but plenty of the other models were. Thank heaven he knew his drugs or cars didn't impress me; therefore, he had no real character to stand on. When he first met me, he tried a few slimy lines but quickly learned I was not like any of his other star-struck models that would let him control or manipulate them. So he kept his distance, and I kept silent as I watched each new model spin in and out of his web.

"I need you for an event tonight," Ken remarked.

"What kind of event?" I asked.

"It is a fashion show at a local boutique. It pays one thousand dollars for three hours. Can you be back here at seven?"

"Yeah, I will do it," I responded, "but I am driving myself there, so I can bounce right after."

"I want all of you girls to go together," he then said.

"Well, I am going on my own terms," I demanded. "I don't really need the money. I am doing you a favor, remember?"

"All right, but the attitude stays here," he said as he slammed the door behind him.

I looked at the clock on the wall that read 3:33 and walked back into the studio.

"You ready to roll, CeCe?" Paige asked.

"Yeah, I am ready to be done with all of this." He didn't know how done with it I really was!

As I positioned myself back into the hammock, I draped my hair across my face and crossed my ankles.

"Hey, Ce, that is a great pose, stay there," Paige shouted.

So I lay there uncomfortably, wondering what the hell I was doing and what was keeping me from getting up.

I just lay in silence while my mind wrestled loudly as the cold air breezed against my nude body. The first flash went off like a sonic boom, and I realized only I had the power to do what was right for me. I stood up and said, "I am sorry, Paige. I can't do this anymore. With each flash of your camera, you are capturing a part of my soul that is no longer for sale. Give my regards to Ken, and tell him I might not make it tonight." I stood up, expecting a fight, but as I stepped out of a glorified fisherman's net, I realized I was breaking strings of confinement all around me.

As I walked away, Paige stood speechless. I grabbed a few things from my dressing room and walked out into the blazing Arizona sun. I wasn't quite sure where I was going, but I knew I was starting to a few steps in the right direction.

Chapter 14

As I reached my car, I realized there was a flyer lying on top of the windshield. I flipped it over and realized it was actually a business card. The fancy cream-colored card had a silver embellished name printed on it that was a little familiar to me. It read, Benjamin Peddalson, Vice President. Ben was a friend of Ken's that ran a multimillion-dollar PR firm. I did not see him at the studio that day, so I wondered how it got there. I opened my door and, with no regard, threw the card on my passenger seat.

On the drive back home, curiosity got the best of me, so I fondled the seat next to me, searching for the card. When I couldn't find it, I took my eyes off the road to scan for it. In a matter of seconds, I looked up to see a truck stopped dead in front of me. All I could do was hit the brakes and pray. My brakes scratched and screeched, trying to go from forty-five to zero in three seconds, but in a moment of chaos, I jerked the wheel hard to the left and ended up in the opposite lane with two cars coming full speed at me. I took my hands off the wheel and stared into my fate. Was this the way I was intended to die?

My life flashed in front of my eyes like reels of tape. A life full of memories I recalled and then flashes of other times I did not.

I saw myself in a lush park pushing a beautiful little girl on a swing. She had brown eyes and black curly hair and something so similar between our smiles. Then I saw me in my thirties with long natural hair, standing over a birthday cake with icing from face to feet. Next I saw me in a white chiffon wedding dress on a black-sand beach, standing hand in hand with an image I could not make out, but all I felt was love. Then my images, as fast as they came, faded back to the reality in front of me.

I braced my hands on top of the steering wheel and thought I was about to die the way God had planned. In amazement, my eyes grew bigger and bigger as I watched the two cars swerve in opposite directions around me. I whipped my head around to find the cars enter their lanes perfectly again as if my car had never existed.

I quickly pushed my foot to the pedal again and sped off in the other direction. When my tires hit the pavement in my driveway, I broke into tears and wondered why. Was I crying because of the situation, the day, or the life that flashed in front of my eyes that I did not recognize? I reached for my bag and realized the little business card that I was searching for was right in front of me. The sunlight hit the silver sketched name, and the glare danced like diamonds on my passenger window. I picked up the card and decided to find out why exactly Ben left it so secretly.

I walked in my house and realized I had three messages blinking on my machine. I hit Play, quickly undressed, and drew a bath. I was always the worst with phone messages. I would listen to half then push Delete, but my ears perked when I heard a very familiar voice on the other side of the line that I hadn't heard for a very long time.

"Hey, Ce, it's Thad. I have something important to tell you. Please call me back."

My heart fell into my stomach. I had avoided him like the plague since my surgery, which was probably close to two years now. Not because I didn't want to see him, but because I didn't want him to see me. They say love is blind, but I think the only blindness lies in the eyes of the betrayer when they realize what they lost.

I hesitated a minute. I needed some time to think about the circumstances of the day. I slipped into a lavender bubble bath. But just as I started to let all my stresses melt away, I heard my answering machine go off again. I sat up and tried to listen, but the male voice sounded mumbled from the bathroom. I am not sure why I let it tear me from the tub, but it did.

I grabbed a cotton towel and wrapped it halfway around me while suds of soap slid down my body; I hurried for the phone. The stranger on the other line had already hung up, so I pushed Play on my machine to see who it was.

"Hello, CeCe, it is Benjamin Peddalson. I left you my contact info on your car earlier, and I wanted to make sure you got it. I am having a little get-together tonight before the fashion show, and I would love it if you were my guest of honor for the event. Everyone is meeting here around six. The car will be here to pick us up around six thirty."

I thought to myself how strange it was that he wanted me to be his guest. Ben had barely shown any interest in me the few times we had been together. I then wondered how in the world he got my home number, but before I could dial Ben back, the phone went off in my hand. Startled, I dropped it to the ground. I bent over to grab it, and in doing that, I lost my towel.

When the phone hit the floor, it landed on the Talk button, and a very familiar voice sounded from the other line. I was in such shock I forgot all about my towel. I stood in the middle of my living room, stark naked, dripping from head to toe.

"Ce, are you there?"

"Hey, Thad," I answered, tripping over my words. "How are you?"

"You are a very hard person to get a hold of," he said in a joking way.

"I am so sorry, I have been . . ." I scrambled to find a word to explain it.

But before I could, Thad jumped in to save me like he always had.

"I know," he said, "busy, busy, busy, that's you, Ce."

"Well," I then interrupted him, "I am never too busy to talk to you. I have just been going through a lot."

"Are you still dancing?"

That question posed such a threat to me.

"Yes, unfortunately, but I am trying to get out."

"Well, I know you can do it. You got out of this town, and if you can do that, you can do anything."

"Thanks," I said, "you will always be my biggest fan." I smiled and realized a total warmth had just washed over me.

"So what is new with you?"

"Well, it is why I called. I am getting married."

And with one sentence, my warmth was washed away. My stomach knotted, and my mouth grew dry while my eyes began to water.

"Ce, are you there."

"Yes, of course, I am sorry. You just caught me off guard. Congratulations, I am so happy for you. Do I know her?"

"Yes, you do, it is Micah Redding. She went to school with your cousin Ky."

"Oh, she is very sweet."

"She doesn't know I am calling you, but I didn't want you to hear it from anybody else."

"I wish you the best. You deserve the best. I am sorry I wasn't the one."

"You don't have to be sorry, Ce. I am happy, and I know one day someone will make you feel the same way."

Lumps of grief started to wallow in my throat, and I knew everything I ate that day was going to come up, so I rushed off the line even though I wanted to savor every word of his because I knew it was probably going to be his last to me. I realized how ironic it was that I was standing completely naked in my living room and my heart was now completely raw. The love of my life, the one stable man I had always counted on, was now gone forever. I could no longer pretend he was going to be my knight in shining armor, because he was the prince in someone else's fairy tale. And when I stood back to examine the picture, Micah made a lot more sense for him, but I couldn't explain that to my heart.

I walked back into my bathroom and stared at the water in my garden tub. I started to ponder all the properties water had. As fetuses we are encased in it, but as humans, in the same situation, we drown in it. We use it to purify, yet we pollute it. My relationship with Thad was a lot like the water, and as I watched it swirl down the drain, it hit me that I was now even emptier than the tub.

I knew I had to get out of the house, or I would just sit and wallow in my sorrow. I ran for the phone and dialed Ben's number. When he answered, I let him know I would be his date for the event, got the directions to his house, and quickly hung up.

I stood in the mirror, trying to apply my makeup, but I was so disgusted with anger and sadness I couldn't even look at myself. My closet was full of colorful appropriate dresses, but nothing but black would suit my mood. I grabbed my favorite black satin mini dress and a pair of tie-up black stilettos and dressed in under five minutes. It was a record for me, and for the first time, I honestly didn't care what I looked like. I threw my hair back in a slick ponytail, fastened a pair of black diamond hoops to my ears, and headed out the door.

I didn't have a far drive to Ben's house, but concentrating on the road seemed to be once again a problem for the day. I turned onto a deserted road that led up one of the many mountains in Paradise Valley. I didn't know it at that time, but it was Ben's own private driveway. When I reached the house, I stepped out of the car and stood breathless at its beauty. The house resembled a castle constructed of stone and glass, and it had an actual mot and draw bridge. There were trees surrounding the driveway that reminded me of weeping willows. I grabbed some lip gloss from my purse and slathered it on my lips as I made the enchanted walk up to the house.

The entry was dimly lit, so I spun a 360, looking for a doorbell. From an outside speaker, I heard a man's voice.

"One minute, CeCe."

Before I had time to figure out how he knew I was there already, the eleven-foot door swung open, and there stood Ben.

"I am so glad you could make it tonight," he said in a very friendly voice.

"Thanks for the invite. I could use some company tonight," I said sternly as I followed him through his exquisite hallway that was covered with musical records engraved with platinum and gold.

"Were you once a musician?" I asked with piqued interest.

"No, I can't hold a note, just an investor. I helped all those groups get their start," he responded.

"That must be such a good feeling knowing you helped so many people accomplish their dreams."

"Well, honestly, that is not why I did it, but huh, I never looked at it like that. I just made a lot of money off of having no musical talent at all."

"Yeah, I guess money is the sad motivation that makes us all tick."

"Funny," he said as he led me to his mustard-yellow couch, "that is one of the reasons I wanted to see you away from Ken. How do you feel about making some extra money that you don't have to give him a cut of?"

I looked at him, and my green eyes saw right through his friendly little smile. He leaned in and grabbed my left knee that was crossed over my right.

"I have a lot of money, and you have a lot of, let's say, talent. We could make a lot of money together."

I politely took his hand off my knee and said, "I am happy with my finances now, thanks."

"Maybe, but don't you want to be done dancing?"

That question posed so much emotion I couldn't even find any words to answer him.

"Let's say I give you three thousand dollars a week, you will be by my side for all my events, promotions, vacations, and other things. I need a beauty with class that will look good on my arm."

"Good on your arm or good in your bed?" I asked.

"Well, honestly, that would be a nice perk for you too."

Disgusted, I got up from the couch and said, "What I call that would be prostitution, and no, that is not a better alternative than dancing. I don't need a sugar daddy, Mr. Peddalson, and frankly, I don't need anything you could possibly give me."

A few degrading comments I heard as I walked out of his front door, but they were only comments of bitterness from a pathetic little boy that always got his way. I didn't think those words could harm me, but as I drove home, I made a U-turn.

Was I just a pretty face, and was this shit constantly going to happen to me?

Did all I have to give was my body? Was this the life I wanted to lead, really?

I made a turn into the camelback mountain preserve, parked my car, and just cried. And in a state of despair I had known before, I got out of my car. I threw my Prada heels to the pavement and began to pace the bottom of the mountain. As I struggled with the evening events, I felt the darkness I knew all too well surround me once again. Here I was, back to beginning, back to the hatred, back to the pain, and back ready to give it all back to the creator. Then it hit me; this was probably just another test.

I thought of the journey I was on and realized I was strong. I was none of the things Ben thought I was. If I was, I would have taken his offer. I wasn't anyone else's fantasy but my own. I wasn't a waste of talent; I just took a detour from my own golden brick road. I was only twenty, and even if it took twenty more years to turn my life around, I was worth it!

I felt the ground underneath me rumble. Earthquakes in Arizona? my mind puzzled. But before my mind could comprehend what was going on, my body was thrown with only a god-like force into the sky.

Chapter 15

I could once again feel myself floating in mid-air, but my mass felt denser. I felt a completeness accompanying my soul, and I felt like I was ascending to a higher plane. I no longer saw utter blackness. I was surrounded in a beautiful purple mist, and I could feel warm beams of light pierce right through me. In the distance I heard angels singing hymns, and I wondered if I was on my way to heaven. A golden brass door began to become clear to me in the distance, and with the wind beneath my feet, I ran for it. Then out of nowhere, I felt like I hit a brick wall.

"It is decision time, CeCe." Othello appeared out of the shadows and with a concerning tone.

"What decision do I have?" I asked.

"You have completed your mission. Now you must decide if you really want to leave Earth. I have given you your true self back. Would you like to enjoy it?"

"Honestly, yes, but I think I will miss you. What if I am not strong enough without your guidance?" I asked.

"I will never be too far away. Just look inside your heart. I will always be there."

"Will I remember any of this?" I suddenly asked, almost knowing the answer.

"One day when your time here is up, you will see me again and see this entire journey, but for your sanity, you will wake up with no memory of me or this experience. However, the courage and self-honesty you have, you earned, so don't be afraid to grab on to new opportunities. You are not just a shell of a person anymore!"

He then placed his gentle hands on top of mine and whispered, "This is only good-bye for now."

And like a plane falling from the sky, my soul fell back into my body. I opened my eyes to find four paramedics desperately trying to revive me. I first noticed the rising sun in the sky. Why was I always out hiking before sunrise? Clearly it was easy to lose your footing in the dark! I wasn't in any real pain except for a dull pain in my left ankle. I tried to stand up but was quickly told to lie still and that a stretcher was coming.

"What happened?" I asked.

One man with an almost too familiar voice said, "Ma'am, you must've fell, but besides a small scrape on your leg, you seem to be in good shape. Are you okay? Do you know your name?"

"I'm fine," I replied. "I'm alive." You can't ask for a better gift than that! "My name is Christine DeMarco"

An EMT with a Southern accent, a gentle smile, brown curly hair, and warm hazel eyes spoke. "Hey, I know you. You sold my sister her condo! I remember your face from your business card!

"Huh?" was all I could remark.

"Because you were knocked unconscious, we are going to take you into the hospital, ma'am for some further testing."

"That is probably best. I don't remember falling at all," I responded. Real estate agent? Yes, that's right, I am a successful real estate agent!

And like a bolt of lightning, memories of a new life began flooding my brain. I once was a girl with no self-respect, no direction, and no sense of purpose; that girl was gone.

I was no longer just a dancer! I had taken a few months off, used some of my contacts for a good reason, went to school, and passed the Arizona Real Estate Sales Exam, and quickly became a leader in my firm. My shrewd business skills and lack of nervousness around high-power men gave me a cutting edge. It wasn't long that I was making a respectful salary and leading a life that I could be proud of. I also had plans to attend college in the fall and get my degree in behavioral psychology and hopefully become a counselor.

My head was still fuzzy over why I was out hiking before sunrise. As I was trying to remember, the nice EMT who rescued me interrupted my thoughts.

"By the way, my name is Nelson. I do not believe we were formally introduced," he said with a friendly smirk. "I will be sure to give your emergency contact information to the hospital staff. I am sure you have a boyfriend or spouse that is worried about you!"

"Actually, if you can just give them my mother's number, she is my 'in case of an emergency' person. I am not involved with anyone at the moment."

A smile flashed across Nelson's face, and he placed his warm hands upon mine. "Well, my lady, would you like a new friend?"

About the Author

Angelia DeSanzo began her love of writing at the early age, publishing several poems and short stories by age eleven. She attended Arizona State University for journalism and mass communications, where she was a columnist and worked in the broadcasting field. She graduated from ASU with a BIS and a master's in education and curriculum. Angelia has been in the education and creative writing field for the last ten years. She is married, with two daughters, and currently resides in Atlanta, Georgia.